THE BLACK HOLE RUN

Kesinachi Ikegwu

THE BLACK HOLE RUN

Published by JDD Books

+447309255086

Book Illustrations by

Nana Agyekum Oppong

heneagyekum@gmail.com

Table of Contents

"JAY!" I shrieked sprinting forward to save him. The ground continued to rumble as the colossal beast chased after us. Jay was being sucked in by the twirling portal while I chased after him, having the beast at my tail and a black hole in front of me. I looked at the black hole and then at the beast and I knew what I had to do...

CHAPTER 1

SCHOOL

"Sam, would you please answer number eleven," asked Miss Miller. Sam…SAM… SAAMM!!!!!! I was suddenly woken up by the loud voice of my teacher. "Yes Miss," I replied, yawning after my short slumber. I couldn't believe that I had fallen asleep in my Maths lesson. Well, I actually could believe it as Miss Miller's lessons were more boring than watching a slug running a 5,000 Mile

Marathon! Before she could say anything else, the bell rang and I dashed out of that classroom like it was on fire. I went straight to my last lesson which was my favourite. We had to learn to control our Powers or as we called them, our SPARK.

My school was made for children who had been gifted with powers. 99% of the children in our school can manipulate fire, lightning, water and ice. The 1 % that didn't have those powers was me. There are 100 people in our school and I am the only one who has psychic abilities. I can read minds of people without sparks, shoot lasers from my eyes, use super strength, fire lightning bolts, teleport, turn invisible and lastly, I can make copies of myself. Yes, I know, our school is pretty cool and weird at the same time but what can I say, we're gifted.

We were tasked by our teacher to be able to defeat the Grand Mage. We had to be in groups of 3.

Everyone in my class gasped. I couldn't believe my ears. There was no way we could go against him. The Grand Mage was the most powerful man on earth who was able to master his SPARK (fire) so well that the colour of the fire turned light blue. Now he could set a whole football pitch on fire with just one blast. Everyone was wandering about and trying to find a strong person to team up with. After a few minutes it was announced that the school board had decided that 50 of the students who went to The SPARK ACADEMY (my school) would continue working at the school, the rest would be kicked out of the school after this task. I knew that I had no time to waste and went straight over to my friends; Mason and Jay. We had to figure out a battle strategy. "Are they insane, why do 50 people have to get kicked out?" Jay shrieked, still not over the surprise. Mason was surprisingly quiet and looked like something was troubling him. I guessed he just didn't want to get kicked out. EVERYONE LINE UP IN YOUR GROUPS OF THREE AND HEAD TO THE TRAINING AREA WHERE YOU WILL FACE THE GRAND MAGE!! This was it; the decider.

CHAPTER 2

THE DECIDER

I stood in line with my team. We had about 20 people in front of us and had our suits on. The training area was gargantuan, it was filled with students who were testing out there SPARK or talking endlessly about how they didn't want to be kicked out. This was definitely the most intense and important event our school has ever had.

Before I knew it my team was being called out to fight the Grand Mage. We had discussed our strategy many times but we all knew that it would be nearly impossible to beat him. "Ready.....GOOOO!!!!" The three of us went three separate ways, I went to the left, Mason went straight and Jay went to the right. Before I could even defend, the Grand Mage hurled a fireball at me. I reacted quickly and dodged it but it skimmed past me by an inch. Even though it didn't hit me it was able to get through the left side of my suit. I knew I couldn't take any more chances so I turned invisible. With Jay and Mason, who had offensive SPARKS, I would have to sneak up on the Grand Mage so I could use my lightning. At the corner of my eye I saw Jay defending against the Grand Mage's attacks but it was no use; his fire blast melted his ice walls in an instant. I had to help him out. I created one clone of myself and we sprinted towards the grand mage. My plan was to get the Grand Mage's attention with my clone and while he is fighting it I would use my invisibility to get behind him and Strike him with a lightning bolt.

Just as I had planned; his attention was off Jay and onto my clone. As I continued to execute my plan I scanned around for Mason and found him lying on the floor knocked out. Even though he was my friend we couldn't get kicked out of the school so I made a clone and sent it to protect him. I couldn't risk him failing the challenge and us being separated. I managed to get behind the Grand Mage and hurled my lightning bolt at him. The lightning spread throughout his body making his skin glow in rays of different colours and he collapsed. No way; I had beaten the Grand Mage.

CHAPTER 3

VICTORY

My team and I were taken to the nurses offices to heal our injuries. Jay and I were dismissed after a few minutes while Mason was being treated after he had been knocked out for 20 minutes. We still couldn't get over the shock that we had beaten the Grand Mage.

After the challenge came to an end; my team was called to have a meeting with the Grand Mage. I guessed it was to congratulate us on our victory. We went to the top of our school building and entered the Grand Mage's office. He greeted us warmly and we were ushered in. The office was cramped. It was filled with piles of books and papers. We sat down and quickly got comfortable. "Boys I am sorry but I have got bad news," the Grand Mage said.

Before we could even react, a Black Hole formed behind us and we were pushed in. In an instant I grabbed Jay's hand and lunged forward. I grabbed onto a chair and looked up; Grand Mage was standing there laughing. I froze and lost my grip.

My eyes fluttered open and I pulled myself up from the ground. My leg was aching and my energy had been drained. I limped towards Jay who was still on the floor. He didn't seem to be heavily injured so he was probably just shaken from the Black Hole. I didn't remember much before being sucked in by the Black Hole. How had he managed to find a black hole. There were only a few Black Holes left in the world and out of the ones left most of them would tear your body into pieces if you went through them. I scanned our surroundings and instantly knew where the black hole had taken us. We were in the Forbidden Land. This was where the first SPARK war took place.

CHAPTER 4

FRIEND OR FOE?

"Did the Black Hole successfully transport them to the forbidden land?" Enquired Mason. The Grand Mage nodded. He didn't know the reason Mason joined him to eliminate everyone who had a SPARK but as he knew a lot about the two strongest people in the school, Sam and Jay, he was useful. The Forbidden Land was the place where the battle between the Lightning

SPARK and the Fire SPARK started. At the end of the war the leaders of each side decided to stop fighting and bring peace.

Mason knew that if someone found out about his partnership with the Grand Mage to eliminate the SPARK community, he would be sent to another dimension for eternity. Despite the consequences, he would not stop until he saw Sam on his knees begging for mercy. Sam and Mason were good friends, but for a long time Mason started to hate him after he surpassed him in terms of using their SPARK. Mason had this planned for a long time and was waiting for the perfect moment to unleash his plan.

Mason watched on the cameras he planted at the forbidden land; Sam had woken up and was kneeling next to Jay who still lay unconscious. Mason laughed to himself. He finally had control over them.

They were his pawns. He looked at the SPARK gadgets he put on them; it detected how high the power of their SPARKS were. As he expected, they were stronger than him. He could not fight them yet but once he finished making his masterpiece, he would be unstoppable.

While Mason and the Grand Mage were laying out their plan; Carl, Sam's brother, had been listening. He couldn't believe his ears. At first he wanted to ambush them but he knew that he would be overpowered as the Grand Mage was there. Suddenly, someone grabbed him by the leg and knocked him out.

"I can't believe he was spying on us," said Mason as he threw Carl into a cupboard.

Now that Mason had caught Carl he could use him to make Sam do what he wanted him to do.

"Where are we?" Jay asked. I told him about how we got here and where we were. I needed to find a way out of here but I didn't know how. The Forbidden land was on the other side of the world so there was no way they could walk back. The only way to get back was to teleport. I could only teleport myself so that would mean I would have to leave Jay by himself.

AHHHHHHHHHHHHH!!!!!

CHAPTER 5

IN A DILEMMA

I turned around quickly and saw a massive beast holding Jay by the neck. I dashed behind the beast and was about to strike it when a hand grew out of its back and grabbed me. I slid out of its grip and darted underneath its legs. I jumped on its back and cut off the arms which were holding Jay with a lightning bolt. Jay fell down and I quickly grabbed him and sprinted away. I darted behind a tree and put him on the floor. "Sam, don't attack the beast again," Jay said.

"What? Why?" Suddenly I remembered seeing a sign on the beast head and I knew why Jay didn't want me to attack it. The beast has been marked by the gods so if we attacked it anymore it would self-destruct. Our only option was to run. Jay got up and we both started sprinting away together. The beast was faster than it looked and caught up with us in no time. We swiftly dogged all the deadly blows while trying not to attack it. Suddenly, the air current changed and we were lifted up from the ground. From the corner of my eye I could see a Black Hole forming. There were two figures coming out of it. It was Mason and the Grand Mage.

They were holding a skinny and frail boy who looked unconscious. I spun around and teleported behind a tree to get a closer look. Suddenly, someone came from behind me and grabbed me. I tried to get out of his grip but I couldn't. I scanned my surroundings and something caught my attention. The boy that was unconscious was my brother. In rage I broke free and charged at Mason. I couldn't believe he was involved in all of this. All of a sudden, the beast had caught up and was right behind me. I looked forward and saw the black hole right in front of me. The Black Hole closed in on me and so did the beast. Before I could do anything, I was sucked in by the Black Hole.

Wake up! Wake up Sam! It's not over yet! The battle isn't over!

Suddenly, I was back. It looked like I was in the middle of the black hole. Purple energy waves swirled all around me. All of a sudden the black hole started closing in. I put both of my hands out on the sides of black hole and pushed as hard as I could. Even with my super strength the black hole kept closing in on me. As the energy swirled around me I knew what I had to do. I let go and propelled myself forward rapidly. I zoomed out of the black hole and landed roughly on the floor.

I looked up to see the Grand Mage and Mason in front of me smirking. I quickly tried to sweep Mason's leg but he dodged it. I hurriedly got up and swung at both of them. Just before they could catch my fist I teleported behind them and struck them both with a lightning bolt. To my surprise the Grand Mage had managed to block my attack with a fireball and Mason absorbed my lightning bolt with one of his own. The Grand Mage hurled a fireball at me and I swiftly dodged it, side stepping. Knowing I couldn't beat them at the same time I charged at Mason knocking him down to the floor. Before I could do anymore damage the Grand Mage grabbed me from behind and flipped me over and in the process slamming me down on the floor. I groaned as I rolled over onto my back.

As quickly as I could, I sprung up from the ground and swung at the Grand Mage knocking him down onto Mason. Leaving no time to waste, I charged my strongest and biggest lightning bolt and struck both of Them. ZAP!!!! They both screamed in agony before they got knocked out.

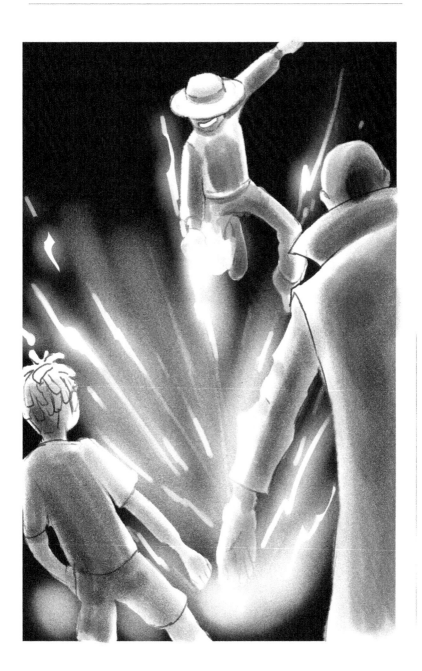

All of a sudden I felt a sharp pain in my chest. Knowing everyone was safe now I fell down too knackered to do anything else.

I had won.

Printed in Great Britain
by Amazon